D0065040

Here's what kids and grown-ups have to say about the Magic Tree House® books:

"Oh, man . . . the Magic Tree House series is really exciting!"
—Christina

"I like the Magic Tree House series. I stay up all night reading them. Even on school nights!"
—Peter

"Jack and Annie have opened a door to a world of literacy that I know will continue throughout the lives of my students."
—Deborah H.

"As a librarian, I have seen many happy young readers coming into the library to check out the next Magic Tree House book in the series."
—Lynne H.

Magic Tree House®

#1: Dinosaurs Before Dark
#2: The Knight at Dawn
#3: Mummies in the Morning
#4: Pirates Past Noon
#5: Night of the Ninjas
#6: Afternoon on the Amazon
#7: Sunset of the Sabertooth
#8: Midnight on the Moon
#9: Dolphins at Daybreak
#10: Ghost Town at Sundown
#11: Lions at Lunchtime
#12: Polar Bears Past Bedtime
#13: Vacation Under the Volcano
#14: Day of the Dragon King
#15: Viking Ships at Sunrise
#16: Hour of the Olympics
#17: Tonight on the *Titanic*
#18: Buffalo Before Breakfast
#19: Tigers at Twilight
#20: Dingoes at Dinnertime
#21: Civil War on Sunday
#22: Revolutionary War on Wednesday
#23: Twister on Tuesday
#24: Earthquake in the Early Morning
#25: Stage Fright on a Summer Night
#26: Good Morning, Gorillas
#27: Thanksgiving on Thursday
#28: High Tide in Hawaii

For a list of Magic Tree House® Merlin Missions and other Magic Tree House® titles, visit MagicTreeHouse.com.

MAGIC TREE HOUSE®

#13 VACATION UNDER THE VOLCANO

BY MARY POPE OSBORNE

ILLUSTRATED BY SAL MURDOCCA

A STEPPING STONE BOOK™

Random House New York

For Louis deWolf-Stein,
who wanted me to
write about Pompeii.

This is a work of fiction. Names, characters, places, and incidents either are the product of the author's imagination or are used fictitiously. Any resemblance to actual persons, living or dead, events, or locales is entirely coincidental.

Text copyright © 1998 by Mary Pope Osborne
Cover art and interior illustrations copyright © 1998 by Sal Murdocca

All rights reserved. Published in the United States by Random House Children's Books, a division of Penguin Random House LLC, New York.

Random House and the colophon are registered trademarks and A Stepping Stone Book and the colophon are trademarks of Penguin Random House LLC.
Magic Tree House is a registered trademark of Mary Pope Osborne; used under license.

Visit us on the Web!
randomhousekids.com
MagicTreeHouse.com

Educators and librarians, for a variety of teaching tools, visit us at
RHTeachersLibrarians.com

Library of Congress Cataloging-in-Publication Data
Osborne, Mary Pope. Vacation under the volcano / by Mary Pope Osborne ; illustrated by Sal Murdocca.
p. cm. — (The magic tree house ; #13) "A Stepping Stone book."
Summary: Their magic tree house takes Annie and Jack to Pompeii just as Vesuvius is about to erupt, and they must find a Roman scroll before everything is covered with burning ash.
ISBN 978-0-679-89050-8 (trade) — ISBN 978-0-679-99050-5 (lib. bdg.) — ISBN 978-0-375-89470-1 (ebook)
[1. Time travel—Fiction. 2. Vesuvius (Italy)—Eruption, 79—Fiction. 3. Pompeii (Extinct city)—Fiction. 4. Tree houses—Fiction.] I. Title. II. Series: Osborne, Mary Pope. Magic tree house series ; #13. PZ7.O81167Vag 1998 [Fic]—dc21 97-39765

Printed in the United States of America 62 61 60 59

This book has been officially leveled by using the F&P Text Level Gradient™ Leveling System.

Random House Children's Books supports the First Amendment and celebrates the right to read.

Contents

1. A Secret Code 1
2. The End Is Near 9
3. Gladiators! 21
4. Scary Things 28
5. Books? Books? 36
6. The End Is *Here* 41
7. The Sky Is Falling 47
8. Nightmare at Noon 54
9. Save Us! 60
10. A Simple Explanation 66

1

A Secret Code

Jack reached into his drawer and took out his secret library card. He held the thin piece of wood and ran his finger over its shimmering letters: **M L**.

"Master Librarian," he whispered.

Jack couldn't believe that he and his sister, Annie, were finally Master Librarians.

He wondered if he should pack the secret card to take on vacation. His family was about to leave for a week in the mountains.

Just then Annie stuck her head into Jack's room.

"Want to check the woods?" she asked.

Every morning, they looked in the Frog Creek woods to see if Morgan le Fay and her magic tree house had returned.

"We can't," said Jack. "We're leaving soon."

"But what if Morgan's there?" said Annie. "What if she's waiting for us?"

"Oh, okay," said Jack. "Let's look fast."

He grabbed his backpack. He threw in his notebook, his pencil, and his secret library card. Then he followed Annie downstairs.

"We'll be back soon!" Annie called.

"Don't go far!" their dad called. "We're leaving in twenty minutes."

"Don't worry, we'll be back in *ten!*" said Annie.

Right, thought Jack. *Five minutes to the woods, and five minutes back.* Even if Morgan sent them on an adventure, they would return at exactly the same time that they left.

Jack and Annie ran out their front door. In the bright morning sunshine, they hurried across their lawn and down the street.

"I had a nightmare last night," said Annie.

"What was it?" said Jack.

"I dreamed fires were burning," said Annie. "Everything was smoky and dark, and the ground was shaking. Do you think it was a warning?"

"Nah," said Jack. "Nightmares never come true."

They left the sidewalk and headed into the Frog Creek woods. The woods were quiet and peaceful. They walked between sunlit trees until they came to the tallest oak in the woods.

"Yay!" said Annie.

There it was—the magic tree house. And Morgan le Fay was waving from the window.

"Hail, Master Librarians," she said.

Jack and Annie bowed playfully.

"At your service," said Annie.

"Then come on up!" said Morgan.

They grabbed the rope ladder and started up. When they climbed inside the tree house, they found Morgan holding a book and a piece of paper.

"I have an important mission for you," she said. "Are you ready?"

"Yes!" they both answered.

Jack's heart pounded. Ever since Morgan had made them Master Librarians, he had been longing for their first mission.

"You know I collect books for Camelot's library?" she said.

Jack and Annie nodded.

"Well, there have been many great libraries lost in history," said Morgan. "And with them, we have lost many wonderful stories."

"That's sad," said Annie.

"It is," said Morgan. "But luckily, with the help of the tree house and you two Master Librarians, some of those stories can be saved. Such as this one—"

Morgan showed them the piece of paper. There was strange writing on it:

Vir Fortissimus in Mundo

"Is that a secret code?" said Jack.

Morgan smiled. "In a way," she said. "Actually, it's the title of a lost story. It's written in Latin, the language of the ancient Romans of Italy."

"Ancient Romans?" said Jack. He loved anything to do with ancient Romans.

"Yes," said Morgan. "This story was in a library in a Roman town. I need you to get it before the library becomes lost forever."

"No problem!" said Annie.

"Do you have your secret library cards?" asked Morgan.

"Yes," said Jack.

"Good. Do not lose them. The right people will know what they mean," said Morgan. "And, as usual, here is a book to help you."

Morgan handed Jack a book called *Life in Roman Times*. The cover showed a Roman town with people wearing tunics and sandals.

"That looks great," said Jack.

"And take this—the name of the story I need," said Morgan. She handed the piece of paper to Jack, and he put it in his pack.

"Remember," said Morgan. "Your research book will guide you. But remember: *In your darkest hour, only the ancient story can save you*. But first you must find it."

Jack and Annie nodded.

"Go now," Morgan said softly. "And don't forget what I just told you."

"Thanks," said Jack. He pointed at the cover of the book on Roman times. "I wish we could go there," he said.

The wind started to blow.

"I almost forgot—I'm going to help you blend in!" Morgan shouted above the wind.

"What do you mean?" shouted Jack.

Before Morgan could answer, the tree house started to spin.

It spun faster and faster and faster.

Then everything was still.

Absolutely still.

"Oh, cool," whispered Annie. "Look at *us*."

2
The End Is Near

Jack opened his eyes. He pushed his glasses into place.

Morgan was gone. And so were Jack's jeans, T-shirt, sneakers, and backpack.

Instead, he had on a white tunic with a belt, sandals that laced up, and a leather bag.

He looked at Annie. She was dressed the same way. Morgan had made them look just like kids in an ancient Roman town.

"I guess this is what Morgan meant," said

Jack, "when she said she'd help us blend in."

"I feel like Cinderella," said Annie. "I like these clothes."

"Yeah," said Jack, although he felt a little as if he was wearing a dress.

Annie looked out the window.

"It's pretty here," she said.

Jack looked with her. They had landed in a grove of trees. On one side of the grove rose a gentle-looking mountain. On the other, a town sparkled in the sunlight.

"I wonder where we are," said Jack. He opened the book about Roman times. He read aloud:

> **Almost 2,000 years ago, on August 24, A.D. 79, the seaside town of Pompeii (pom-PAY) was a typical Roman town. Many Romans went there on their**

vacation. They built large houses called villas and planted groves of olive trees along the slopes of a mountain called Mount Vesuvius (vuh-SOO-vee-us).

Annie kept looking out the window as Jack pulled out his notebook and pencil. He wrote:

Vacation in Pompeii
August 24, A.D. 79
houses called villas

Jack looked out the window again.

"It does look like a nice place to go on vacation," he said.

"We must have landed in one of the olive groves," said Annie.

"Yeah, and that town must be Pompeii," said Jack.

He looked in the opposite direction. "And that mountain must be Mount Vesuvius."

Annie shivered. "That name sounds scary," she said.

"Really?" said Jack. "Not to me." He looked down at his notes.

"Hey! Did you feel that?" said Annie.

"What?" Jack looked up.

"The ground shook. I heard it rumble, too," said Annie.

Jack frowned. "I think you were just dreaming again," he said.

"No, I wasn't," said Annie. "Something feels wrong about this place. I really think we should go home now."

"Are you nuts?" said Jack. "We have to

find that lost story for Morgan. Besides, I've always wanted to see a Roman town."

He threw his notebook and the Roman book into his leather bag. Then he went down the rope ladder.

"Come on!" he called when he stepped onto the ground.

Annie just stared down at him.

"Don't be chicken," he said. He pushed his glasses into place. "Come on. It'll be fun."

Annie still didn't move.

What's wrong with her? Jack wondered. *Usually* I'm *the worried one.*

"Come on," he pleaded. "We can't let Morgan down."

Annie let out a big sigh. "Okay, but we'd better find that story fast," she said. Finally she climbed down the rope ladder.

The sun was bright and hot as they took off between the olive trees.

With Mount Vesuvius at their backs, they headed for the town of Pompeii.

"That's weird," said Annie. "I don't hear any birds."

She was right. The grove was strangely silent.

"Don't worry about it," said Jack. "Maybe they're all at the beach. Come on—let's go over that bridge."

He led the way to a small wooden bridge that crossed a narrow stream. But when they got to the stream, they found it had dried up.

"That's *really* weird," said Annie.

"Don't worry," said Jack. "It just means there hasn't been much rain."

They crossed the bridge and stepped onto a busy street. It was paved with stone.

People were buying things in the open shops that lined the street. Some looked rushed and busy. Others moved slowly. Kids walked with their parents. Groups of teenagers talked and laughed.

They don't seem very different from people shopping in Frog Creek, Jack thought.

Except for the clothes, of course.

"How will we ever find the ancient lost library?" said Annie, glancing around.

"I don't know," said Jack. "Just be on the lookout."

They walked past shops that had huge jars in them. When Jack looked closely, he saw that they were filled with grain, dried fruit, and olives. Meat hung from the ceilings of some of the stores.

They passed a noisy tavern where people were eating and drinking. A young man played a stringed instrument.

"See, there's nothing to worry about," said Jack. "This place isn't all that different from our time."

"It's not that," said Annie with a worried look.

"See, there's a barbershop and a shoe shop," said Jack, pointing.

A boy was getting his hair cut by the barber. A girl was trying on a new pair of sandals with her mother.

"It is kind of like home," Annie agreed.

They kept walking, until they passed a bakery filled with freshly baked flat breads.

"That bread is like pizza," said Annie, smiling.

"Yeah," said Jack.

The good smells from the bakery made him feel even more at home. Jack looked at Annie. She was still smiling as they walked on.

Soon they came to a large square filled with people, carts and horses, and more shopping stalls.

"Honey cakes! Stuffed dates! Peacock eggs!" sellers called.

Farmers were selling grapes, garlic, and onions. Fishermen were selling all kinds of fish. A few people stood on boxes, giving speeches to small crowds.

"Hey, I bet this is the forum!" said Jack. He reached in his bag for his book. He flipped through it until he found a picture of the square. He read:

> **The center of a Roman town was called a forum. The forum was the main place where people met to sell goods and discuss politics.**

"I was right!" said Jack. He pulled out his notebook. He wrote:

forum = center of town

"Jack," whispered Annie. "Jack!" She tugged on his tunic. "Look."

Jack glanced up. Annie nodded toward an old woman who was staring straight at them.

She wore a black cloak. Her gray hair was tangled and wild. She seemed to be missing her teeth.

The woman pointed a bony finger at Jack and Annie.

"The end is near!" she said in a raspy voice. "Go home, strangers!"

"Yikes," said Annie.

"We'd better get away from her," said Jack, "before people wonder who we are."

He put away his notebook. Then he and Annie hurried away. The old woman cackled behind them.

3

Gladiators!

Jack and Annie hid behind a fruit stall. They waited for a moment, then peered around the corner.

"I don't see her," said Jack.

"Who was she?" asked Annie.

"I don't know. But she looked nuts to me," said Jack.

"What's the book say about her?" said Annie.

"She won't be in there," said Jack.

"Just look," said Annie.

Jack sighed and pulled out the book again. To his surprise he found a picture of the old woman. He read aloud:

> **In Roman times, there were people who could see into the future and warn others about what they saw. These people were called soothsayers.**

"See? She wasn't nuts," said Annie. "She was giving us a warning. Just like my nightmare."

"Don't pay attention to that stuff," said Jack. "Soothsayers are from olden times. People from our time don't believe in them."

"Well, I do," said Annie. "I'm *sure* something bad is about to happen."

Jack sighed. "Come on, we have to keep

going. We have to find the lost library. Then we'll leave at once."

"We'd better," said Annie.

They left the fruit stand and kept walking through the forum. Soon they came to a large building. Crowds were streaming in and out of it.

"Is *that* a library?" said Annie.

"Let's look," said Jack. He looked in the Roman book. He found a picture of the building and read aloud:

> **Most people in Pompeii did not have a bathtub at home, so they went daily to the Public Baths. Not only did people wash at the baths, but they also swam, played sports, and visited with their friends.**

"That sounds like going to the pool," said

Annie. "But it's not a library. Let's keep walking."

They kept walking, until soon they came to a fancy building with large columns.

"Is *that* a library?" said Annie. Jack found a picture of the building and read aloud:

The people of Pompeii believed that many gods and goddesses ruled the world. This is the Temple of Jupiter, their chief god. In this temple, they prayed to Jupiter and offered him gifts. Today, we call the stories about Jupiter and other gods and goddesses "myths."

"My teacher read myths to us," said Jack. "I remember stories about Hercules and Apollo."

"Yeah, my teacher read them, too," said Annie. "I like stories about Venus and Medusa."

"Hey, maybe the story we're looking for is a myth," said Jack.

"Right," said Annie. "Come on, hurry. Let's keep looking."

They left the forum and turned onto a wide street. Jack gasped. In front of them was an incredible sight.

Tall warriors with *huge* muscles were walking in a line. They wore fancy helmets and carried heavy shields.

Soldiers, thought Jack.

Then he saw that the warriors' feet were

chained together, and guards walked with them.

"*Gladiators!*" he whispered.

4

Scary Things

Jack pulled out his book and found a picture of the strong men. He read aloud:

> **Gladiators were slaves or criminals who fought in the amphitheater (AM-fuh-thee-uh-ter). They were forced to fight each other or wild animals like lions or bears. The people of Pompeii thought a gladiator fight was great fun.**

"That's not fun!" said Annie. "No wonder I think it's weird here."

"No kidding," said Jack. "That's not like our time at all."

Jack and Annie watched as the guards led the gladiators away. They went toward a building that looked like an outdoor stadium.

"That must be the amphitheater," said Jack. "Let's check it out."

"Oh, all right, but it's not a library," said Annie.

He and Annie started up the street toward the amphitheater. A large crowd had gathered near the entrance. Men and women cheered as the gladiators marched inside.

Jack and Annie started to follow them, but a guard held up his spear.

"No children allowed," he said stiffly. "Run along now."

"Yes, run along! Run for your lives!" came a raspy, hissing voice.

Jack and Annie whirled around. It was the soothsayer. She was waving her bony finger at them.

"Oh, no! Her again!" said Jack. "Let's get away from here." He started to take off.

"Wait!" said Annie. "I want to talk to her!"

"Are you crazy?" said Jack.

But before he could stop her, Annie ran up to the soothsayer.

Jack watched from a distance as the woman talked to Annie.

"Jack, come here! Quick!" called Annie.

"Oh, brother," said Jack. He sighed and went over to Annie and the soothsayer.

"Tell him," said Annie.

The woman fixed her gaze on Jack.

"All the streams of Pompeii have dried up," she said.

"Remember the stream near the olive grove?" said Annie.

"So what?" said Jack. "Maybe they just need rain."

"No," said Annie. "There're more scary things. Tell him."

"All the birds have flown away," the soothsayer said.

Jack just stared at her.

"She said that all the rats left, too," said Annie. "And the cows are making strange noises!"

"But why?" said Jack.

"The sea is boiling hot," the old woman said. "And the ground shakes and speaks."

"See, I told you!" Annie said to Jack.

"But why are these things happening?" Jack asked the soothsayer.

"Because the end is near," she whispered hoarsely.

"We have to leave now!" said Annie.

"But what about the library?" said Jack.

"What library?" the soothsayer asked.

"Show her the story title, Jack," said Annie.

Jack took the piece of paper from his bag. He showed the Latin writing to the soothsayer. "A book with this title is in a library in this town," he said.

"So?" the old woman said.

"So we have to save it!" said Annie. She pulled out her secret library card.

The soothsayer stared for a moment at the card and the shimmering letters on it. Then she smiled warmly at Jack and Annie.

"Yes, I understand now," she said. "The only library I know is in the house of Brutus." She pointed to a large villa at the end of the street. "Look there. Quickly."

"Will Brutus mind?" said Jack.

"Brutus and his household are all in Rome," the soothsayer said. "That is merely their vacation villa."

"But we can't just go in and take something of theirs," said Jack.

The old woman shook her head sadly. "After today, there will be *nothing* left in Pompeii," she said. "Nothing at all."

Jack felt a chill go down his spine.

"Go and get what you came here for," said the soothsayer. "Then leave at once."

"Thanks!" said Jack. He grabbed Annie's hand. "Come on!"

"Thanks!" Annie called to the old woman. "You should leave, too!" she added.

Then Annie and Jack started running to the vacation villa. They ran as fast as they could.

5
Books? Books?

Jack and Annie ran up to the front entrance of the villa. Jack pushed the door open.

"Go in. Hurry," said Annie.

They slipped into the main hall.

"Hello!" Annie called.

There was no answer. The place seemed empty.

The main hall had a large opening in the ceiling. Below it was a small stone pool filled with water. Jack looked at it carefully.

"Oh, I bet rain comes through the hole," said Jack. "Then it lands in that pool so they can use it for their water."

He started to take out his notebook to make a note.

"There's no time, Jack!" said Annie. "We have to look in all the rooms for books!"

"Okay, okay, calm down," said Jack. He put away his notebook and followed Annie.

"Books? Books?" she said, peering into a room off the hall. She moved to the next room. "Books? Books?" Then she moved on to the next.

Jack trailed behind her. Even though she had already checked the rooms, he took a quick peek in each of them. He wanted to see what a house in Roman times looked like. He'd write notes later.

The first two rooms had wooden beds. The walls had pictures painted on them. The floors were covered with tiny pieces of colored stone.

The third room had a low table with silver dishes on it. Three sloping couches were placed around the table. The couches were covered with pillows.

"This must be the dining room," said Jack. "People from Roman times lay down on couches while they ate. Did you know that?"

He looked around for Annie. Where was she?

"Jack! Come here!" Annie called.

Jack followed her voice. She was in a garden off the dining room. It had a stone patio, palm trees, and grape vines. In the middle was a pond with a mermaid fountain. Goldfish swam in the water.

"Look, there's another room!" said Annie. She moved to the door of a room off the garden.

She opened the door and peeked inside.

Jack looked with her. Along the walls of the room were long shelves with rolls of paper on them.

"Rats!" said Annie. "No books." She closed the door. "No books in this *whole* villa. Let's get out of here."

"Just a minute," said Jack. "I have an idea."

He pulled out his book on Roman times. He found a section called WRITING. He read:

> **Romans used pens made of small reeds. Their ink came partly from the black ink of octopuses. They wrote their "books" on scrolls of papyrus (puh-PI-rus) paper.**

"Aha!" said Jack. "That's a library of scrolls! I bet our ancient lost story is in there!"

6

The End Is Here

Jack threw open the door to the room of scrolls. He and Annie rushed in and ran over to the shelves.

Jack pulled out the piece of paper with the Latin title on it:

Vir Fortissimus in Mundo

"Okay," he said. "We have to find the scroll with this title."

They began frantically unrolling scrolls

one by one. They were all handwritten in Latin.

"Here it is!" said Annie.

She held up a scroll. The words at the top matched the ones on their paper.

"Yay," said Jack. "I wish I could read Latin so we could find out what the story is."

"Don't think about it now!" said Annie. "Let's go!"

Annie handed the scroll to Jack, then started out of the room.

"Come on," she said. "Bring it!"

"I just want to check and see what the story's about," said Jack.

He put the scroll in the leather bag. Then he flipped through the book on Roman times, looking for a picture of the ancient scroll. In the middle of the book, he found a picture of a volcano erupting over a town.

Under the picture was written:

> **For 800 years, Mount Vesuvius was a peaceful mountain, rising above the town of Pompeii. Then, at noon on August 24, A.D. 79, it erupted into a deadly volcano.**

"Oh, *no*," whispered Jack. "August 24, A.D. 79—that's *today!* Oh, man, what time is it?" He looked around wildly. "Annie!"

She was gone again.

"Annie!"

Jack grabbed the leather bag. Then, clutching the book, he tore out of the scroll room.

"*Annie!*" he cried.

"What?" Annie appeared at the door to the dining room.

"V-v-volcano!" stuttered Jack.

"*What?*" said Annie.

"It's—it's coming—a volcano—at noon!" said Jack.

Annie gasped.

"What time is it?" cried Jack.

"So *that's* what the soothsayer meant!" Annie said. "The end *is* near."

"What time is it?" Jack asked again. He looked around the garden.

He saw something near the mermaid fountain.

"A sundial!" he said. "That's how the Romans told time!"

Jack and Annie raced to the sundial.

"What time does it say?" said Annie.

"I don't know," said Jack.

His hands shook as he turned the pages

of the book. He stopped on a picture of a sundial. It showed examples of different times. Jack looked back and forth from the page to the real sundial in the garden.

"Here!" he said. He had found the one that matched. Jack read the writing under the picture:

> **The shadow on the sundial can hardly be seen at noon.**

"Oh, man," he whispered. He looked at Annie. "The end isn't near; the end is *here*."

Just then he heard a terrible blast. It was the loudest sound he had ever heard.

7

The Sky Is Falling

The next thing Jack knew, he was lying on the stone patio. The patio stones were trembling. A rumbling sound came from the ground.

Jack raised his head. Annie was on the ground, too.

"You okay?" said Annie.

Jack nodded.

Everything was shaking and crashing down around them—pots, plants, the mermaid fountain. Water from the goldfish pond sloshed onto the patio and Jack and Annie.

They both jumped up just as roof tiles began falling into the garden.

"We better get inside!" said Jack.

He grabbed his leather bag. Then he and Annie stumbled into the scroll library.

Giant cracks split the stone floor as Jack and Annie ran to a window and looked out.

Glowing rocks were bursting through the sky above Mount Vesuvius. The whole top of the mountain had blown off.

"What's happening?" said Annie.

"I'll check—" said Jack. He pulled out the Roman book. He read aloud from the section about the volcano:

> **When a volcano erupts, hot melted rock called "magma" is pushed to the surface**

of the earth. Once it gets outside the volcano, it's called "lava."

"Lava! That's like burning mud!" said Jack.

"It covers everything!" cried Annie.

Jack kept reading:

There was no running lava from Mount Vesuvius. The magma from the volcano cooled so fast that it froze into small grayish white rocks called pumice (PUM-iss). A pumice rock is very light and has holes like a sponge.

"That doesn't sound *too* bad," said Annie.

"Wait, there's more," said Jack. He read on:

A great cloud of pumice, ash, and burning rock shot miles into the air. When it rained down on Pompeii, it

completely buried the town.

"Oh, man," said Jack. "This is a major disaster!"

"It's getting dark," said Annie.

Jack looked out again. A thick black cloud was spreading over the earth like an umbrella. The sun vanished as the sky turned smoky gray.

"That must be the cloud of pumice and ash!" said Jack.

Just then the ground trembled again. Chunks of plaster from the ceiling fell on the scrolls.

"We have to get out of here!" said Annie.

They ran from the scroll library into the garden. Ash and pumice began to fall.

"We have to cover our heads!" said Jack.

They hurried from the garden into the dining room.

"Look! Pillows!" said Annie. "Let's put them on our heads!"

They hurried to the couches beside the table and each grabbed a pillow.

"Tie it around your head with your belt!" said Jack.

They both pulled off the belts from around their tunics. Then they tied on the pillows, like giant hats.

A chunk of ceiling crashed down near them.

"Let's get out of here!" said Jack.

They stepped over pieces of fallen roof tiles and ran into the main hall. They pushed open the front door.

A blast of heat and dust nearly knocked

them over. And when they stepped outside, pumice rained down onto their pillow hats.

"Run!" cried Annie.

They ran from the vacation villa into the dark, burning streets.

8

Nightmare at Noon

In the distance, fire burst from Mount Vesuvius. Burning rocks and fiery ash fell from the sky.

The hot, dusty air smelled like rotten eggs as Jack and Annie rushed down the street. In the forum, everyone—shoppers, soldiers, gladiators, fruit sellers—was running in every direction.

Stalls had collapsed. Carts were sliding.

Jack froze. He didn't know where to go.

"That way!" shouted Annie.

Jack followed her as they ran past the Temple of Jupiter. Its mighty columns had fallen, and its walls were crumbling.

They ran past the Public Baths just as its roof caved in.

"Which way now?" shouted Annie.

"The tree house is in the olive grove!" Jack said as they kept running.

"The olive grove and the bridge are near the street with all those open shops!" said Annie. "Remember the bridge?"

Jack looked up at the erupting mountain. A red-hot cloud billowed over it. Fires burned on its slopes.

"Head in the direction of Mount Vesuvius!" he said. "It was behind us as we came into Pompeii."

"Right!" cried Annie.

So while others ran *away* from Mount Vesuvius, Jack and Annie ran *toward* it.

On the street with the open shops, baskets and broken jars rolled over the cracked stones.

Jack and Annie ran past the bakery and the shoe shop. They ran past the butcher shop and barbershop. All the shops were empty. Their owners had fled.

The closer they got to the volcano, the more the ground trembled. The darker and dustier it got.

"This is just like my nightmare!" cried Annie.

Jack choked on the rotten fumes. His eyes watered.

"Look! The olive grove!" shouted Annie.

"The tree house is just over there! Come on!"

Jack could hardly see, but he followed Annie. They left the street and ran to the dried-up stream near the olive grove.

"Where's the bridge?" cried Annie.

They looked around wildly. *The bridge had vanished.*

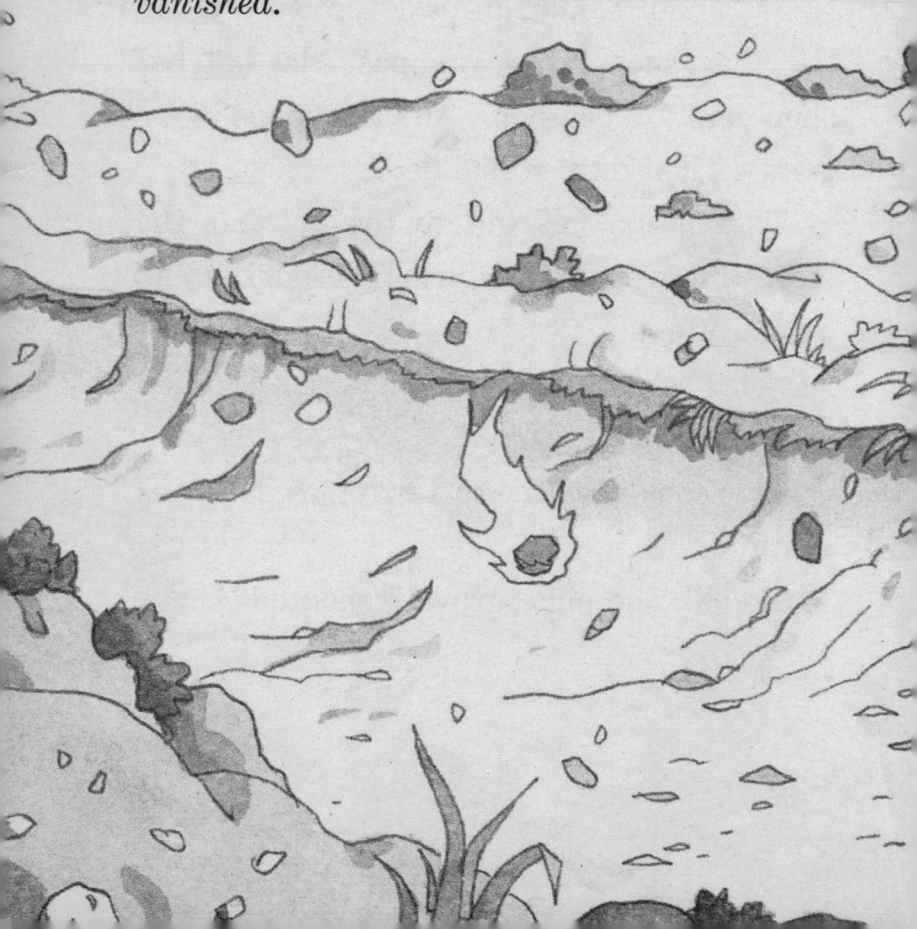

9
Save Us!

"The bridge must have caved in!" cried Annie.

They stared at the dried-up stream. Pumice had piled up in huge drifts, like snow.

"We'll have to get through that stuff to get across!" said Jack.

He and Annie slid down the bank onto the piles of pumice. As they started to move across it, more and more fell.

Jack tried to move through the millions of warm, grayish white pebbles. But he was trapped.

"I'm stuck!" cried Annie.

"Me too!" said Jack.

"Remember what Morgan said!" said Annie.

At the moment, Jack couldn't remember anything. He was too tired and dazed.

"'In your darkest hour, only the ancient story can save you!'" cried Annie. "Where's your bag?"

Jack lifted his bag into the air, above the sea of pumice. Annie grabbed it and pulled out the ancient scroll. She held it up to the dark sky.

"*Save us, story!*" she shouted.

Jack felt himself sink deeper and deeper

into the pumice. Suddenly he heard a deep voice say, "Rise, son!"

Then someone lifted Jack up into the air.

A great flash of fire lit the dusty darkness. In the red light, Jack saw the biggest, strongest man he'd ever seen in his life. The man looked like a gladiator—but even bigger than the ones they had seen earlier.

He held Jack with one hand and Annie with the other. He placed them both on the other bank of the stream.

"Run!" the giant gladiator boomed. "Before it's too late!"

Jack and Annie didn't stop to ask any questions. Together, they charged through the olive grove.

They jumped over fallen branches. They leaped over great cracks in the earth. Finally they came to the tree with the magic tree house.

They grabbed the rope ladder and scrambled up to the tree house.

"Where's the Pennsylvania book?" Jack shouted. He was too blinded by ash and dust to find the book that always took them home.

"I've got it!" cried Annie. "I wish we could go there!"

Jack felt the tree house start to spin.

It spun faster and faster and faster.

Then everything was still.

Absolutely, wonderfully, peacefully still.

10
A Simple Explanation

Jack didn't move. He had never been so tired in all his life.

"Breathe," said Annie.

Jack gulped in cool, clean air. He opened his eyes. He couldn't see a thing.

"Take off your glasses," said Annie. "They're filthy."

Jack took off his glasses. The first thing he saw was his backpack. The white tunics and lace-up sandals were gone. So were their pillow hats and the leather bag.

Jack let out a long, deep breath. As he cleaned his glasses on his shirt, a voice came from behind him. "I'm *very* glad to see you safe and sound."

Morgan le Fay stood in the corner of the tree house. She looked as lovely and mysterious as ever.

"Happy to be home?" she asked.

Jack nodded. The sound of the erupting volcano still echoed in his ears.

"It—it was pretty scary," he said in a hoarse voice.

"I know. But you were truly brave," said Morgan. "You witnessed a famous event in history. Nowadays, scientists study the remains of Pompeii to find out more about Roman times."

"I feel bad for all those people," said Annie.

"Yes," said Morgan. "But most of the people of Pompeii *did* escape. The city wasn't completely buried by ash until the next day."

"We were almost trapped," said Annie. "But we asked the ancient story to save us. Then a huge gladiator helped us."

Jack reached into his pack. He breathed a sigh of relief. The scroll was still there! He took it out. It was covered with dust and ashes.

"Here's the story," said Jack.

He handed it to Morgan.

"I am deeply grateful," she said softly. "You risked everything to bring this to me. I can never thank you enough."

"Don't worry about it," said Jack. He

didn't want Morgan to know how scared he had been.

"Yeah, no problem," said Annie.

Morgan smiled. "You are amazing Master Librarians," she said. "Do you think you're up to rescuing another ancient story?"

"Yes!" said Annie.

"Now?" said Jack. Actually he was a little tired now.

Morgan laughed. "No. Take a nice vacation. Come back two weeks from today. Then you will take a trip to ancient China," she said.

"Ancient China? Wow," said Annie.

"Oh, man," said Jack.

"Go home now and rest," said Morgan. She handed Jack his pack.

"Thanks," he said. "Bye."

"Bye," said Annie.

Morgan gave them a little wave. Then Annie and Jack left the tree house and headed down the rope ladder. When they reached the ground, Jack looked up.

"Morgan," he called. "What is that story about—the one we just rescued?"

"It's called *The Strongest Man in the World*," said Morgan. "It's a lost tale about Hercules."

"*Hercules?*" said Jack.

"Yes, he was one of the heroes of the Greeks and the Romans," said Morgan. "He was a son of Jupiter."

"Oh, wow. *Now* I get it," said Annie.

"I'm taking it back now to Camelot's library," said Morgan. "Everyone will be so excited to read it, thanks to you." She waved to them. "Good-bye for now!"

As she waved, the wind began to whirl. The tree house began to spin. In a blur of shadow and light, Morgan and the magic tree house were gone.

Jack and Annie started walking through the woods.

"Get it? Get it?" said Annie.

"Get what?" said Jack.

"We were saved by Hercules!" said Annie. "We asked the story to save us—and *Hercules* appeared!"

"That's not possible," said Jack. "It was just some gladiator guy. The story of Hercules is a *myth*. That means he never really lived."

They left the woods and started up their street.

"I know it's a myth," said Annie. "But I have a simple explanation."

"What?" said Jack.

"Hercules is a myth to people in *this* time," said Annie. "But in Roman times, lots of people believed he was real. So, since we were in Roman times, he was real to us."

"I don't know . . ." said Jack.

"Did you ever hear the saying?" said Annie. "*When in Rome, do as the Romans do.*"

Jack laughed. "Yeah." He looked up at the sky. "Thanks, Hercules," he said softly, "whatever you are."

"Jack! Annie!" their dad called from their front porch. "Time to go!"

"Oh, brother, I forgot," said Jack.

"Yeah, I hope nothing exciting happens on *our* vacation," said Annie.

"Yeah," said Jack. "I hope it's really, *really* boring."

"Hurry!" their dad said.

"Coming!" they called.

Then they took off running for home—and a restful vacation.

More Facts for You and Jack

1) Pompeii was forgotten after it was buried in ash and pumice. In 1594, the ruined city was discovered by workmen who were digging a tunnel. Later, a nearby town called Herculaneum was also discovered. It had been buried by boiling mud after the volcano erupted. Many things from everyday life have been uncovered in both Pompeii and Herculaneum. Recently, a library of scrolls was found.

2) The language of the ancient Romans was called Latin. Many words in the English, French, and Spanish languages come from Latin. For example, *liber* means "book" and *libri* means "books" in Latin. The word "book" in Spanish is *libro* and in French is *livre*. In English we have the word "library."

3) Mount Vesuvius erupted in the year A.D. 79. The letters "A.D." stand for the words *anno Domini*. *Anno Domini* means "in the year of the Lord" in Latin, which refers to the year Jesus Christ was born—about 2,000 years ago.

4) The Romans took their name from the city of Rome, which was the capital of their empire. Rome is now the capital of the country of Italy.

5) In A.D. 79, the Romans had a powerful army. They ruled all of Western Europe, the Near East, and North Africa.

6) Hercules is the Roman name for the hero from the Greek myths known as Heracles. After the Romans conquered ancient Greece, they adopted many of Greece's heroes and gods and goddesses. Heracles—who became Hercules—was one of them.

Here's a special preview of

Magic Tree House® Fact Tracker

Ancient Rome and Pompeii

Help Jack and Annie track down facts about ancient Rome!

Available now!

Excerpt copyright © 2006 by Mary Pope Osborne and Natalie Pope Boyce. Illustrations copyright © 2006 by Sal Murdocca. Published by Random House Children's Books, a division of Penguin Random House LLC, New York.

Gladiators

Gladiators were trained in hand-to-hand combat. Most were prisoners or slaves, but some were freemen who got paid for fighting.

Severus uses a net to snare his opponent and a trident to stab him.

Gladiators usually fought to the death. But if an especially brave fighter was wounded, the emperor could spare his life. The eager crowds bet on their favorites. Some gladiators got as much attention as rock stars do today!

Marcus fights with a sword and a shield.

3

The Roman Military

In AD 103, huge crowds lined the streets of Rome. They'd come to see the return of Emperor Trajan after his victory over the Dacians.

Trumpets rang out. People moved forward to catch a glimpse as standard-bearers strode by carrying flags with symbols identifying their units. Hundreds of soldiers paraded by, loaded with treasures from the defeated people. Next a bedraggled group of prisoners shuffled by, dragging their chains.

And finally Trajan himself rode by in a golden chariot pulled by four prancing horses. The Roman army had returned in triumph once again!

Men ages 17–46 could be soldiers.

For over 400 years, Rome had one of the greatest armies the world has ever seen. At the peak of the empire, 300,000 soldiers swore absolute loyalty to the emperor and to their generals. The Roman Empire would not have been possible without the army.

The Legion

Roman soldiers belonged to fighting groups made up of about 6,000 men. These groups were called *legions* (LEE-junz). Legions were divided into eighty-man units called *centuries* (SEN-chuh-reez). Centuries were commanded by battle-hardened officers called *centurions* (sen-CHUR-ee-unz).

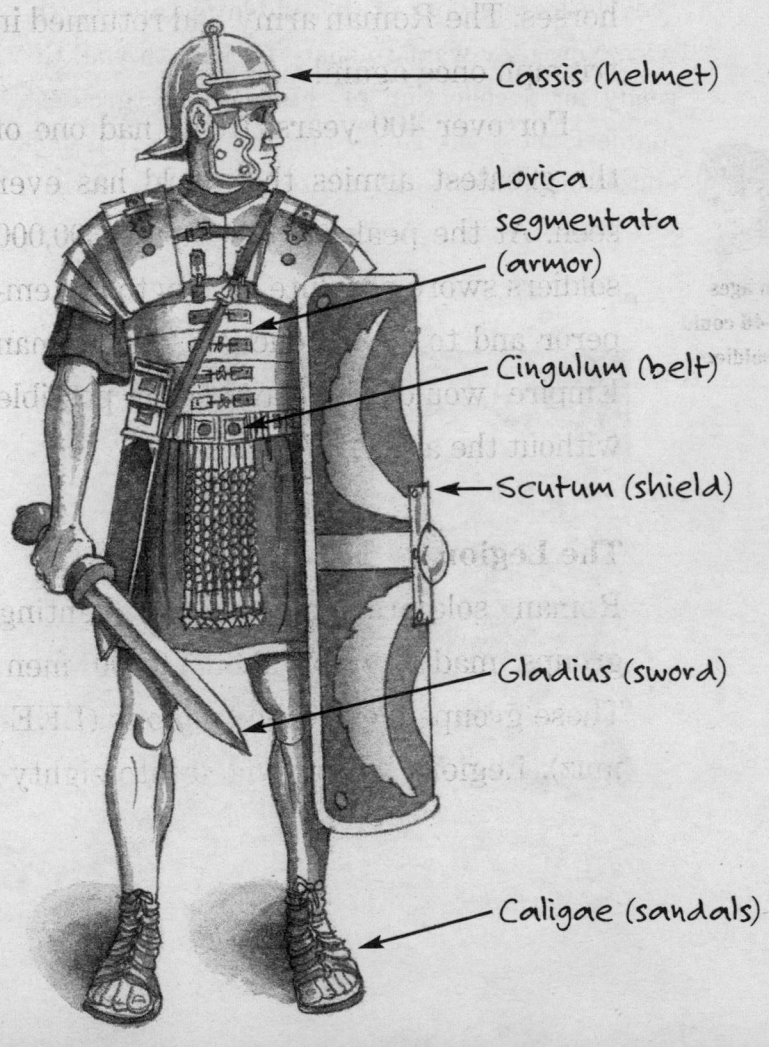

Enough cool facts to fill a tree house!

Jack and Annie have been all over the world in their adventures in the magic tree house. And they've learned lots of incredible facts along the way. Now they want to share them with you! Get ready for a collection of the weirdest, grossest, funniest, most all-around amazing facts that Jack and Annie have ever encountered. It's the ultimate fact attack!

Don't miss

Magic Tree House® #14

DAY OF THE DRAGON KING

Jack and Annie visit ancient China to save a precious book from being burned. . . .

Available now!

Magic Tree House®

#1: Dinosaurs Before Dark
#2: The Knight at Dawn
#3: Mummies in the Morning
#4: Pirates Past Noon
#5: Night of the Ninjas
#6: Afternoon on the Amazon
#7: Sunset of the Sabertooth
#8: Midnight on the Moon
#9: Dolphins at Daybreak
#10: Ghost Town at Sundown
#11: Lions at Lunchtime
#12: Polar Bears Past Bedtime
#13: Vacation Under the Volcano
#14: Day of the Dragon King
#15: Viking Ships at Sunrise
#16: Hour of the Olympics
#17: Tonight on the *Titanic*
#18: Buffalo Before Breakfast
#19: Tigers at Twilight
#20: Dingoes at Dinnertime
#21: Civil War on Sunday
#22: Revolutionary War on Wednesday
#23: Twister on Tuesday
#24: Earthquake in the Early Morning
#25: Stage Fright on a Summer Night
#26: Good Morning, Gorillas
#27: Thanksgiving on Thursday
#28: High Tide in Hawaii

Magic Tree House® Merlin Missions

#1: Christmas in Camelot
#2: Haunted Castle on Hallows Eve
#3: Summer of the Sea Serpent
#4: Winter of the Ice Wizard
#5: Carnival at Candlelight
#6: Season of the Sandstorms
#7: Night of the New Magicians
#8: Blizzard of the Blue Moon
#9: Dragon of the Red Dawn
#10: Monday with a Mad Genius
#11: Dark Day in the Deep Sea
#12: Eve of the Emperor Penguin
#13: Moonlight on the Magic Flute
#14: A Good Night for Ghosts
#15: Leprechaun in Late Winter
#16: A Ghost Tale for Christmas Time
#17: A Crazy Day with Cobras
#18: Dogs in the Dead of Night
#19: Abe Lincoln at Last!
#20: A Perfect Time for Pandas
#21: Stallion by Starlight
#22: Hurry Up, Houdini!
#23: High Time for Heroes
#24: Soccer on Sunday
#25: Shadow of the Shark
#26: Balto of the Blue Dawn
#27: Night of the Ninth Dragon

Magic Tree House® Super Edition

#1: World at War, 1944

Magic Tree House® Fact Trackers

Dinosaurs
Knights and Castles
Mummies and Pyramids
Pirates
Rain Forests
Space
Titanic
Twisters and Other Terrible Storms
Dolphins and Sharks
Ancient Greece and the Olympics
American Revolution
Sabertooths and the Ice Age
Pilgrims
Ancient Rome and Pompeii
Tsunamis and Other Natural Disasters
Polar Bears and the Arctic
Sea Monsters
Penguins and Antarctica
Leonardo da Vinci
Ghosts
Leprechauns and Irish Folklore
Rags and Riches: Kids in the Time of Charles Dickens
Snakes and Other Reptiles
Dog Heroes
Abraham Lincoln
Pandas and Other Endangered Species
Horse Heroes
Heroes for All Times
Soccer
Ninjas and Samurai
China: Land of the Emperor's Great Wall
Sharks and Other Predators
Vikings
Dogsledding and Extreme Sports
Dragons and Mythical Creatures
World War II

More Magic Tree House®

Games and Puzzles from the Tree House
Magic Tricks from the Tree House
My Magic Tree House Journal
Magic Tree House Survival Guide
Animal Games and Puzzles
Magic Tree House Incredible Fact Book

MARY POPE OSBORNE
MAGIC TREE HOUSE
Continue the adventure with Jack and Annie!
Use your exclusive code below to unlock special content at MagicTreeHouse.com/exclusives.
MERLIN
1268

CALLING ALL ADVENTURERS!

Join the
MAGIC TREE HOUSE®
KIDS' ADVENTURE CLUB

Members receive:

- Exclusive packages delivered throughout the year
- Members-only swag
- A sneak peek at upcoming books
- Access to printables, games, giveaways, and more!

With a parent's help, visit MagicTreeHouse.com to learn more and to sign up!

© 2016 Mary Pope Osborne. Magic Tree House is a registered trademark of Mary Pope Osborne; used under license. Illustrations © 2016 by Sal Murdocca.

MagicTreeHouse.com

BRING MAGIC TREE HOUSE TO YOUR SCHOOL!

Magic Tree House musicals now available for performance by young people!

Ask your teacher or director
to contact
Music Theatre International
for more information:
BroadwayJr.com
Licensing@MTIshows.com
(212) 541-4684

ATTENTION, TEACHERS!

The Magic Tree House **CLASSROOM ADVENTURES PROGRAM** is a free, comprehensive set of online educational resources for teachers developed by Mary Pope Osborne as a gift to teachers, to thank them for their enthusiastic support of the series. Educators can learn more at MTHClassroomAdventures.org.

© 2014 Mary Pope Osborne. Magic Tree House is a trademark of Mary Pope Osborne, used under license. Illustrations © 2014 by Sal Murdocca.